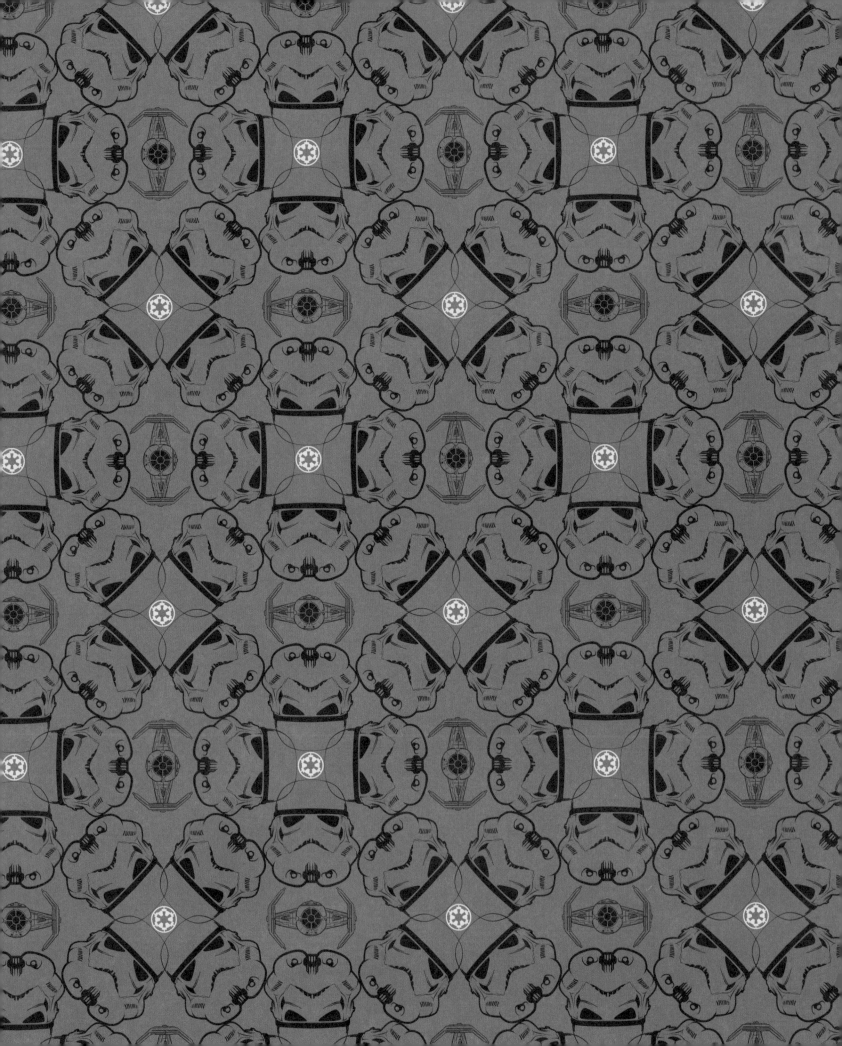

SCARED, DARTH VADER?

by Adam Rex

Disney
LUCASFILM
PRESS

LOS ANGELES · NEW YORK

FOR HENRY . . . I AM YOUR FATHER. —A. R.

The characters in this book were drawn and painted in Photoshop with KyleBrush brushes, then superimposed over photographs of a swamp created with paper, clay, paint, moss, glue, sticks, stones, foam, sponge, and schmutz.

Designed by Adam Rex and Scott Piehl

Printed in the United States of America
First Edition, July 2018 10 9 8 7 6 5 4 3 2 1
Library of Congress Control Number on file
FAC-038091-18138
ISBN 978-1-4847-0497-4

Visit the official *Star Wars* website at:
www.starwars.com.

IT'S MIDNIGHT. THERE'S A FULL MOON!

THAT IS NO MOON.

WHATEVER. ARE YOU SCARED, DARTH VADER?

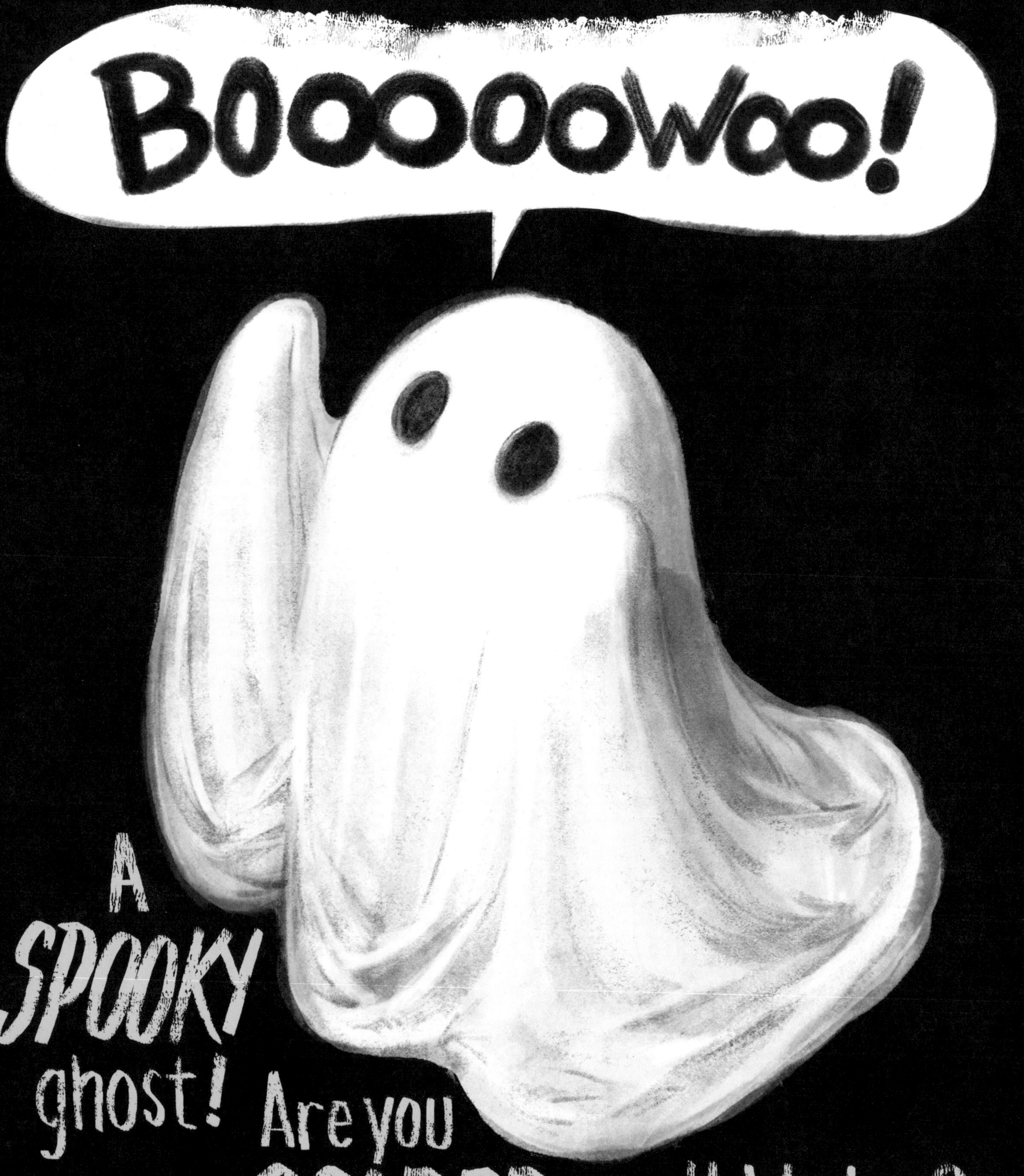

A *SPOOKY* ghost! Are you *SCARED*, Darth Vader?

IS THIS THE GHOST OF OBI-WAN KENOBI?
Um...
OR YODA? IT IS SHORT LIKE YODA.
I think it's just a ghost.
NEXT.
POKE

She's also a witch! Are you SCARED, Darth Vader?
LET ME GUESS— SHE BITES YOU?
No, she casts spells! She could curse you!

Are you afraid of spiders?

NO.

Black cats?

NO.

Public speaking?

NO.

The dark?

IS THAT A JOKE?

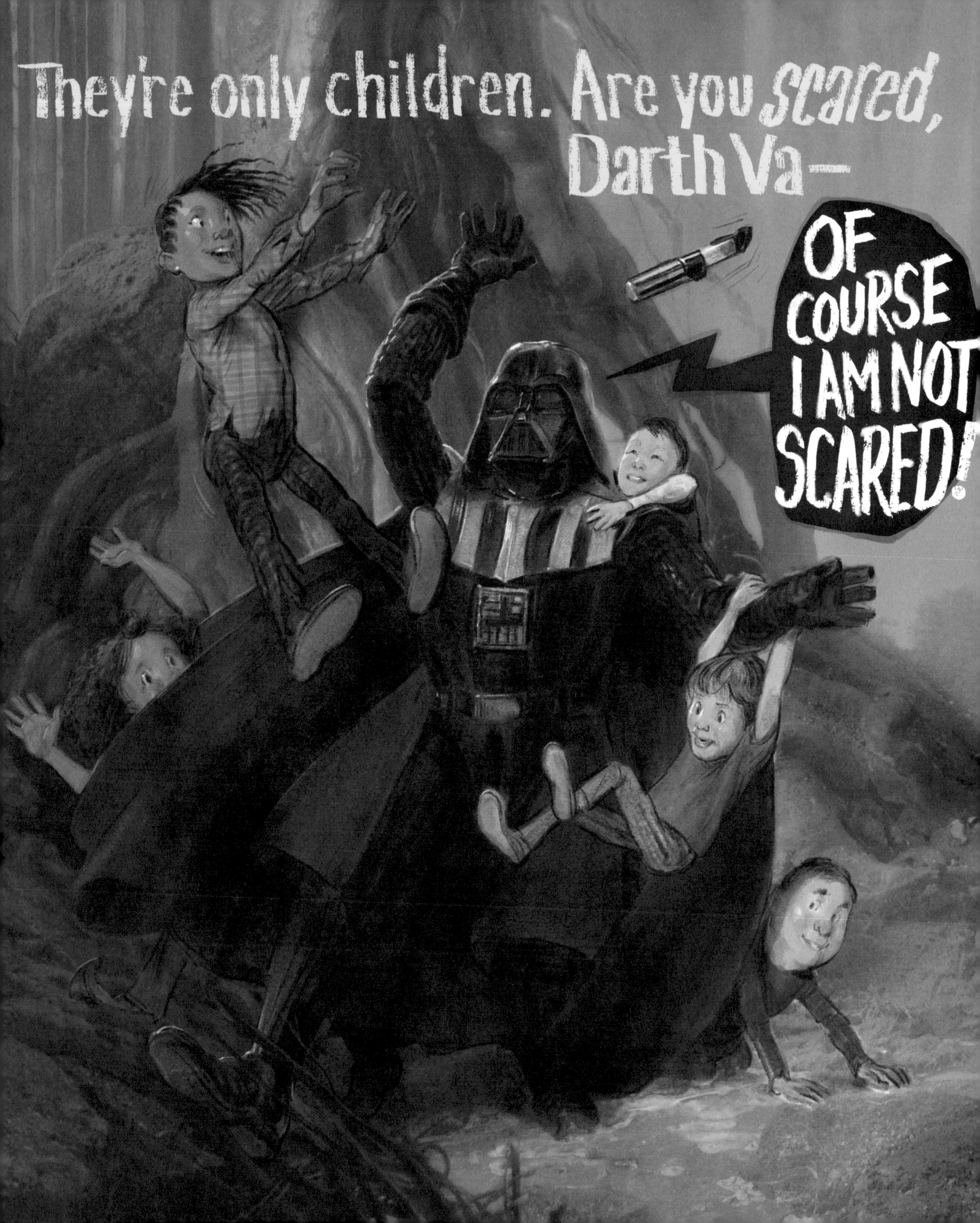
They're only children. Are you *scared*, Darth Va—
OF COURSE I AM NOT SCARED!

Then you wouldn't mind if *more* children came to play?

pew pew pew

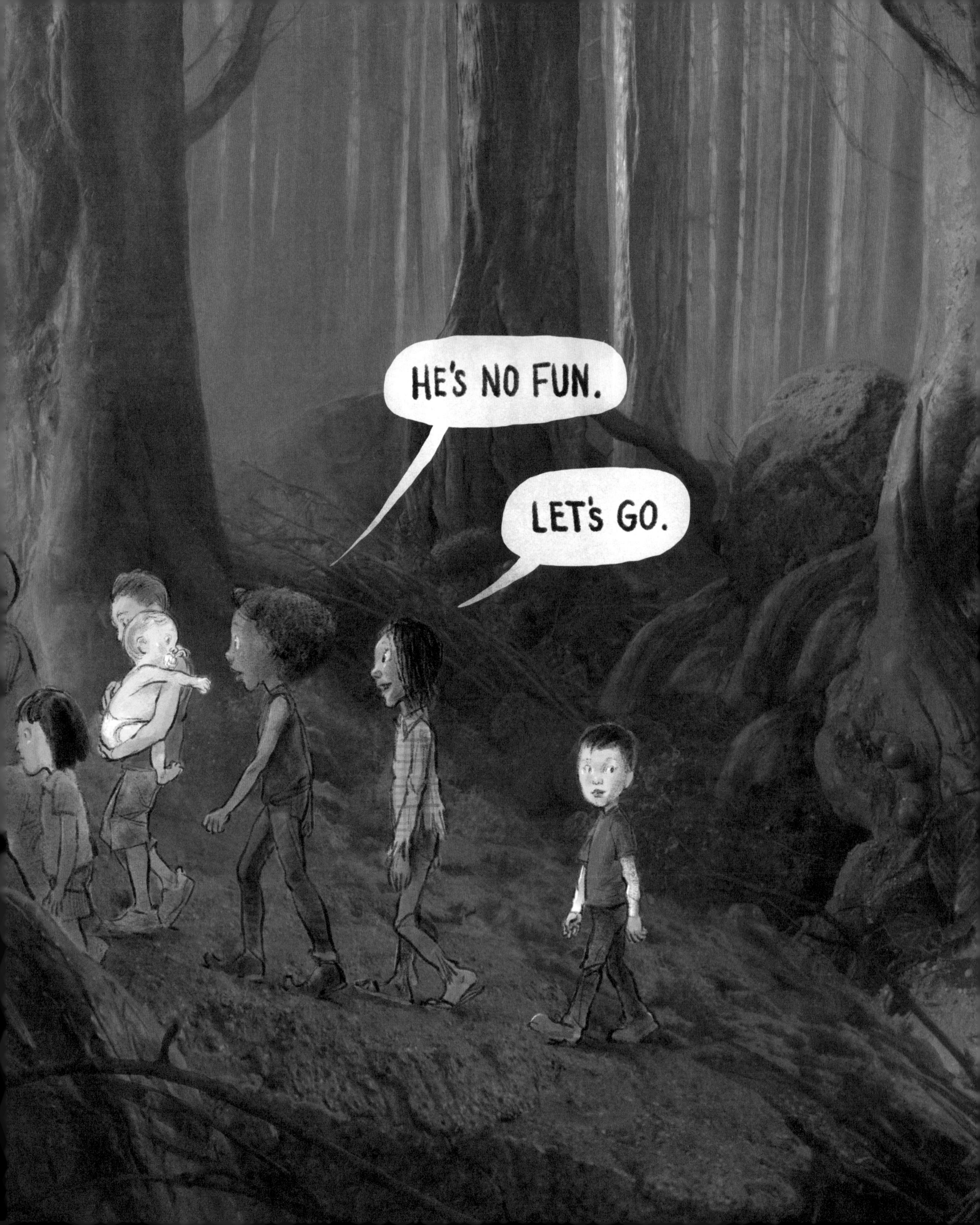
HE'S NO FUN.
LET'S GO.

But look, Darth Vader. There's still one kid left — the one who's about to close the book.

What's the matter?
LISTEN TO ME, CHILD!
YOU DO NOT WANT TO TURN THE PAGE!

Wow, I guess this kid has the power to trap you inside the book!

Almost like you're frozen in carbonite, or whatever.

CHILD!

THE POWER OF THE DARK SIDE COMPELS YOU!
JOIN ME AND TOGETHER WE CAN RULE THE GALAXY!

only one page left.
Now are you
SCARED,
Darthy?-

OF COURSE
I AM!

AHHH! STOP! DO NOT TURN THE-

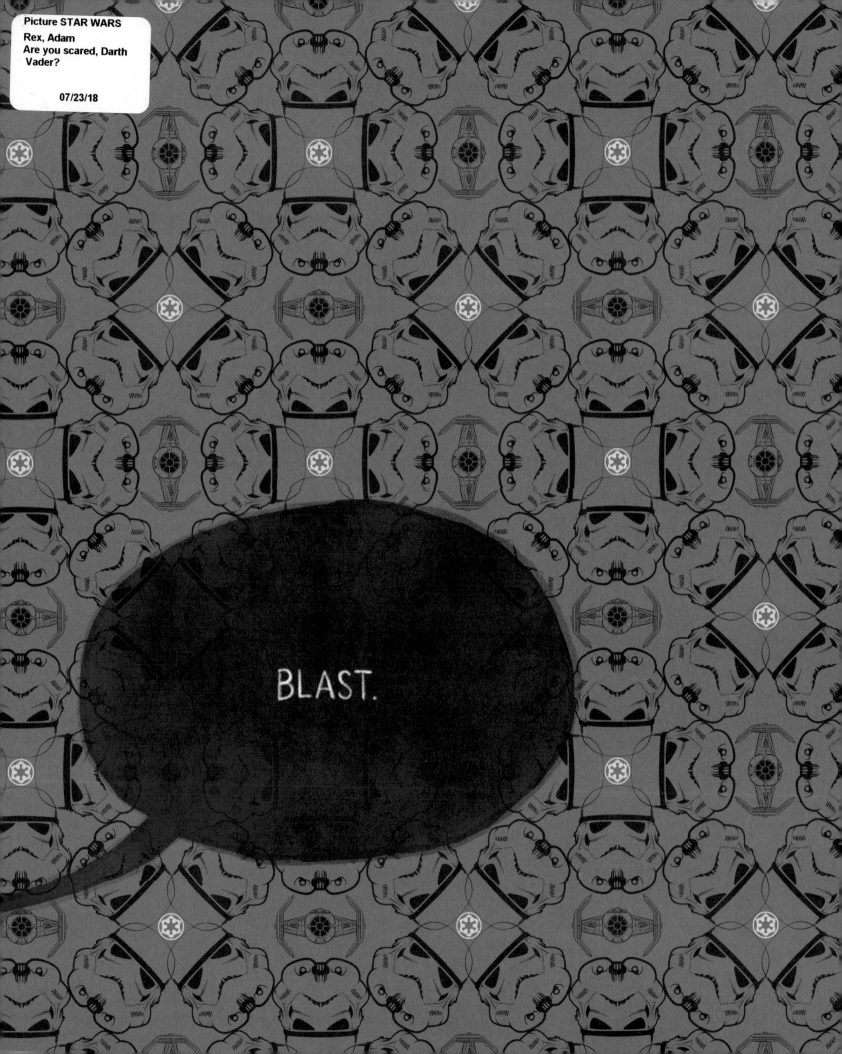